To Eli
for all your
dreams come true
All my heart—
Mama

If You're Afraid of the Dark
Remember the Night Rainbow

by Cooper Edens

GREEN TIGER PRESS
Published by Simon & Schuster
New York   London   Toronto   Sydney   Tokyo   Singapore

GREEN TIGER PRESS
Simon & Schuster Building, Rockefeller Center
1230 Avenue of the Americas, New York, New York 10020
Copyright © 1979 by Cooper Edens
All rights reserved including the right of reproduction
in whole or in part in any form.
GREEN TIGER PRESS is an imprint of Simon & Schuster.
Manufactured in the United States of America

10   9   8   7

Library of Congress Cataloging-in-Publication Data
Edens, Cooper. If you're afraid of the dark,
remember the night rainbow / by Cooper Edens.
p.   cm.   Summary: Presents advice for a variety of situations,
including what to do if the sky falls, the bus doesn't come,
the sun never shines again, and there is no happy ending.
I. Title.   [PZ7.E223If 1991]   [E]—dc20   91-15823   CIP

ISBN: 0-671-74952-8

If tomorrow morning the sky falls...

have clouds
  for breakfast,

If night falls...

use stars
for streetlights,

If the moon gets
stuck in a tree...

cover the hole
in the sky with
a strawberry.

If you have butterflies
in your stomach ...

ask them into
your heart.

～

If your heart catches
in your throat...

ask a bird
how she sings.

If the birds
Forget their songs...

listen to
a pebble
instead.

If you lose
a memory...

embroider
a new one to
take its place.

If you lose the key...

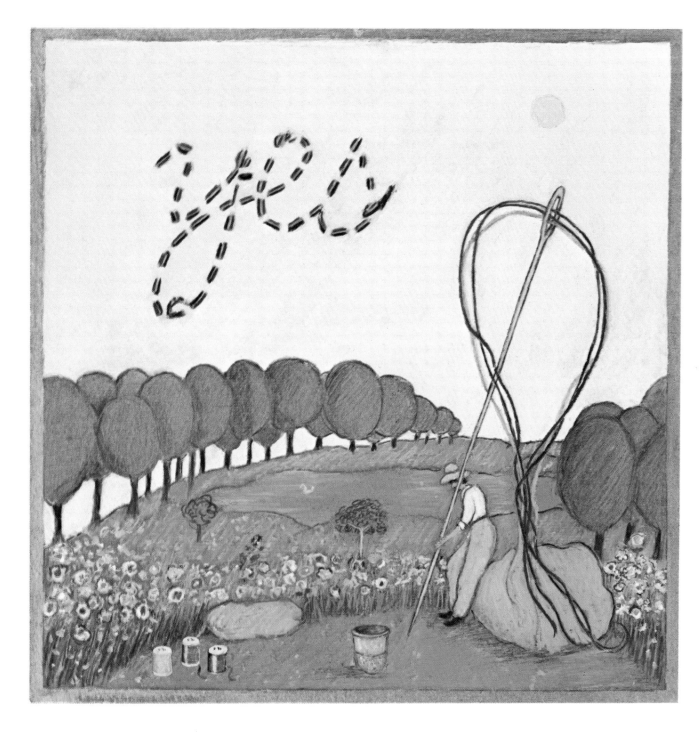

throw away
the house.

If the clock stops...

use your own hands
to tell time.

If the light goes out...

wear it around
your neck and
go dancing.

If the bus doesn't come...

catch a fast cloud.

If it's the last dance...

dance backwards,

if you find your
socks don't match ...

stand in a
 Flowerbed.

If your shoes don't fit...

give them to the fish
in the pond.

If your horse needs shoes...

hold fireflies
in your hands
to keep warm.

❧

If you're afraid
of the dark ...

let him use his wings.

If the sun
never shines again...

remember the
night rainbow.

If there is no
happy ending...

make one out of
cookie dough.

Color Separation by
Sunset Graphics
San Diego, California

Calligraphy by
George Weinberg-Harter